Right Where You Are Now

written by lisa montierth • illustration by ashley burke •  CRAIGMORE CREATIONS

Library of Congress Catalog Number 2011933497

ISBN: 978-0-9844422-2-5

First Edition, September 2011

Made and Printed in Portland, OR

www.craigmorecreations.com

Lisa Montierth is a freelance writer, a nature lover,
and an Idaho native. Her favorite dinosaur is the brontosaurus.

Ashley Burke is an illustrator and motion designer living in Portland, Oregon.
Her favorite animal is a bunny rabbit. Visit her website at www.ashleyburke.com.

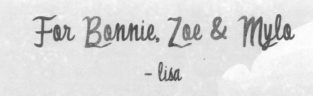

For Bonnie, Zoe & Mylo

- lisa

For my g-ma,
i love you

-ashley

Right where you are now, night is here. The yellow moon shines down on a quiet house.
Soon, everyone will be sleeping. But once...

There were no houses. There was only a salty sea. Fish lizards called ichthyosaurs and carnivorous plesiosaurs swam through coral reefs. Warm rains fell into the shallow waters. The world looked very different, right where you are now.

Right where you are now, an icy mountain stands quietly in the mist. But once...

The mountain was pushed up from the ground by the moving earth. Other mountains were created with it, and they stood together in a line. These mountains grumbled and shot out lava, right where you are now.

Right where you are now, quiet streets twist together. But once...

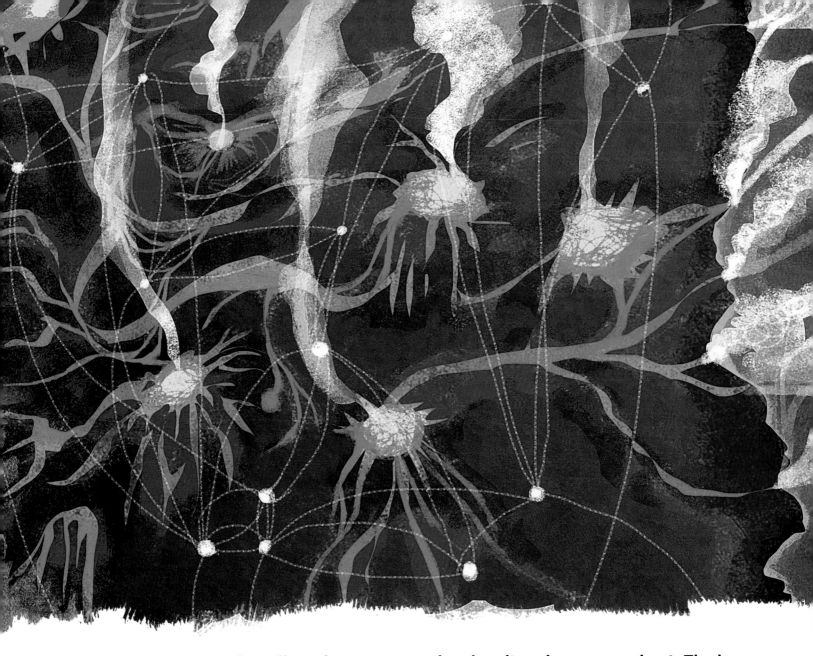

It was lava that twisted for miles. Fissures opened and molten rivers poured out. The lava flowed across the land and melted things down, right where you are now.

Right where you are now, flowers bud and grow, then fall and sleep with the changing seasons. But once...

There was only one warm, rainy season. Rainforest covered much of the earth. Green vines twined and magnolia could bloom all year long, right where you are now.

Right where you are now, dry maple leaves rustle along the dark streets. But once...

Forests grew wild ginkgo. Metasequoia stood tall with cypress and willow and yew.
These trees grew in a mucky swamp, right where you are now.

Right where you are now, a caterpillar spins a cocoon in a patch of grass.
But once...

Grasslands blanketed the earth. Dog, bear, rhinoceros, and sloth lived on the warm prairie. Grasshopper grazed, and so did merychippus, right where you are now.

Right where you are now, a bluebird nests in a tall oak. But once...

There were no bluebirds in the sky. Megacerops, the Thunder Beast, lumbered through the woodlands. Uintatherium grazed on leaves and grass. Many animals, strange and wonderful, have come and gone, right where you are now.

Right where you are now, an orange cat stretches and closes his bright eyes.
But once...

There was nimravid, a creature with long teeth. Nimravid was not a cat, but he looked like one. He stalked his prey on the wild land, right where you are now.

Right where you are now, tall skyscrapers stand dark in the heart of the city.
But once...

This land was under water. Huge waves from a lake in the North cut a path to the sea and made channels in the rock and soil. Melting ice changed the Earth, right where you are now.

Right where you are now, people are sleeping in their warm beds. But once...

Humans slept in caves.

They gathered berries and nuts to eat and they hunted wild animals with tools made of rock and bone. They made fire and wore animal skins to stay warm. They drew pictures of the things they saw on the rocks.

Some humans made canoes from wood and paddled out to an island to live. They made sandals from sagebrush and bark to protect their feet. Humans were very resourceful, right where you are now.

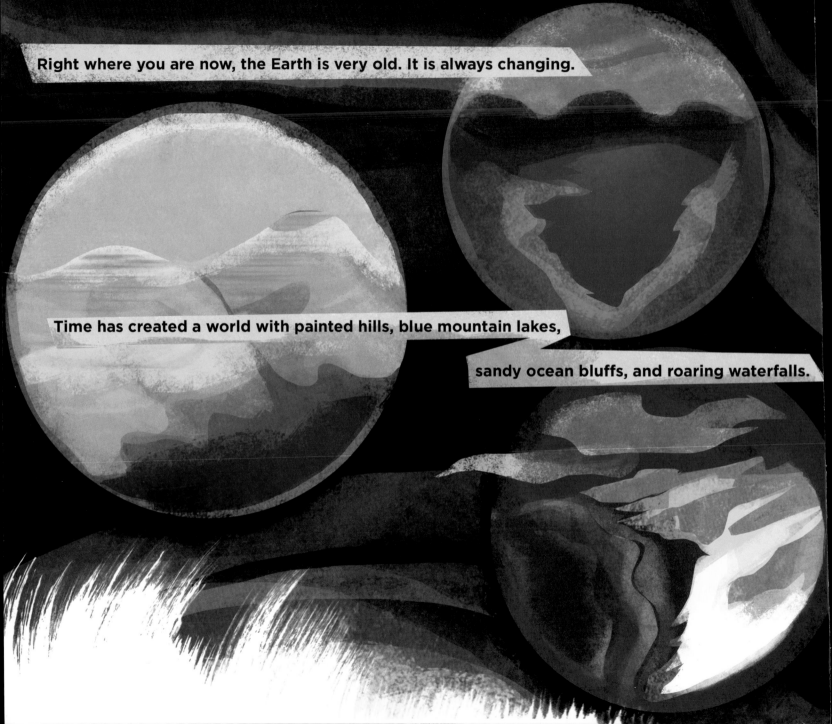

Right where you are now, the Earth is very old. It is always changing.

Time has created a world with painted hills, blue mountain lakes,

sandy ocean bluffs, and roaring waterfalls.

The world looks different every day, right where you are now.

Rain falls and volcanoes erupt, while glaciers freeze and thaw.

Right where you are now, night is here. The yellow moon shines down on a quiet house.

Soon, everyone will be sleeping. And then...

It will be dawn. The sun will rise and warm the land. Birds will sing in the bright new day. Can you imagine what may come to be, right where you are now?

The End

The Visual Dictionary

Ichthyosaur [ik-thee-uh-sawr]
This marine reptile lived in the oceans from 245 to 90 million years ago.
Though it looks like a dolphin or a fish, it is not related to either.

Plesiosaur [plee-see-uh-sawr]
This carnivorous aquatic reptile swam in the seas from 210 to 65 million years
ago. Because of its four flippers and massive body, it was a slow but
exceptionally maneuverable swimmer.

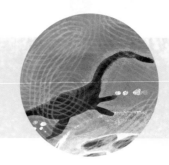

Merychippus [mare-ee-kip-us]
An ancestor of the modern horse, Merychippus had three toes instead of the
modern one-toe hoof of today's horse. It lived throughout North America from
20 to 10 million years ago.

Megacerops [meg-uh-ser-ops]
Its name means "large horn face." From 38 to 34 million years ago, this beast thundered across the land eating plants and grasses.

Uintatherium [u-in-ta-the-ri-um]
This large animal grazed on aquatic vegetation. Its long canine teeth were used for protection and may have aided in cutting water plants from their deep roots. It lived from 45 to 40 million years ago in the Eocene period.

Nimravid [nim-ra-vid]
Though this animal looks a lot like a saber-toothed cat, it is not related to any of the felines. Subtle differences in bone and teeth structure have caused paleontologists to place this animal in a separate family of animals related as much to hyenas as cats. It lived from 37 to 5 million years ago.

Flood Basalts
Millions of years ago, in places that are now called Siberia, India, South Africa, and the USA, there were giant flows of lava called flood basalts. Rather than spewing from volcanic mountains, flood basalts ooze out of long cracks in the ground, covering thousands of square miles of land and cooling into plateaus and mountains.

Ice Age Floods
At the end of the last ice age, between 15,000 and 8,000 years ago, there were gigantic floods in North America as the ice melted into enormous amounts of fresh water. The melting ice and flowing water caused climatic changes and carved many of the landscapes that we know today.

Acknowledgments

Concept by David Shapiro
Project direction by Erica Melville
Production assistance by Caroline Knecht

Made and Printed in Portland, OR